THE WIND IN THE WILLOWS

The Wild Wood

*It had been a fine spring day when the Water Rat had taken
Mole for his first row on the river.
Ratty had packed a picnic and as they began their feast, two
of the Rat's friends had appeared, Otter and Badger.
Ever since that day, Mole had been curious about the
mysterious Badger.*

Mole was longing to meet Mr. Badger. He was the kind of person who everyone knew about, but nobody ever saw.

"Badger will turn up some day or another, and then I'll introduce you!" promised the Rat.

"Couldn't you ask him to dinner or something?" said Mole.

"He wouldn't come," replied Ratty simply. "Badger hates coming to dinner and all that sort of thing."

"Well then, supposing we go and call on him," suggested Mole.

"Oh, I'm sure he wouldn't like that at all," said the Rat, quite alarmed. "Besides, we can't because he lives in the very middle of the Wild Wood. He'll come here some day, if you wait long enough."

But Badger never did come. The summer was long over and winter was on its way. Mole waited and waited, still longing to meet this mysterious grey Badger who lived by himself in the middle of the Wild Wood.

So one winter's day, when Mole had a good deal of spare time on his hands, he decided to go out by himself and explore the Wild Wood - and perhaps meet Mr. Badger.

Ratty was dozing in an armchair in front of a blazing fire when Mole slipped quietly out of the warm parlour and into the open air.

The afternoon was cold and the countryside bare and leafless.

Mole felt quite cheerful as he made his way to the Wild Wood which lay before him, low and threatening.

There was nothing to frighten him at first. Twigs crackled under his feet, logs tripped him, fungi on stumps looked like faces and startled him for a moment, but it was all fun and exciting. It led him on and he went deeper into the wood where there was less light and the trees made ugly, frightening shapes.

Everything was very still now. Dusk was falling and the light was fading.

Then the faces began. First a little evil wedge-shaped face, looking out at him from a hole, and then vanishing.

He quickened his pace, telling himself not to imagine things!

Then suddenly, Mole seemed to see a face in every hole. He quickly dived off the path and plunged deep into the wood itself.

Then the whistling began. Very faint and shrill it was, and far behind him. Then it got louder and this time it was in front of him. Poor Mole was quite alone, he was far from help and the night was closing in.

Then the pattering began. It seemed to be the pat-pat-pat of little feet. But was it in front or behind?

As he stood still to listen, a rabbit came running hard towards him, "Get out of this, you fool, get out!" the Mole heard him mutter.

In panic, he began to run too. He bumped into things, fell over things and darted under things. At last he hid in the deep, dark hollow of an old beech tree.

As he lay there panting and trembling and listening to the patterings outside, he understood why Ratty had tried to keep him away from the Wild Wood.

Meanwhile, the Rat was just waking from a long nap in front of the fire. He looked around for Mole, but Mole was not there and the house seemed very quiet.

"Moley!" called Ratty several times, and getting no answer, got up and went into the hall.

The Mole's cap was missing and so were his galoshes.

Ratty left the house and found Mole's footprints outside in the mud leading straight to the Wild Wood.

The Rat looked very grave. He went back indoors, strapped a belt around his waist, put a pair of pistols into it, took a stout stick and set off for the Wild Wood.

It was already getting dark when he reached the first trees and he rushed straight into the wood.

Here and there, wicked little faces popped out of holes, but vanished at the sight of the brave Rat. The whistling and the pattering died away and all was still.

Ratty made his way through the dark wood, all the time calling out cheerfully, "Moley! Moley! Moley! Where are you? It's me, it's old Rat!"

Then at last, he heard a little voice saying, "Ratty, is that really you?"

The Rat crept into the hollow beech tree and found Mole, exhausted and trembling. "Oh Ratty!" he cried. "I've been so scared, you can't think!"

Mole was greatly cheered by the sight of Ratty's stick and his pistols and he soon began to feel bolder.

"Now then," said the Rat, "we must get moving while it's still light."

"Ratty," said Mole, "I can't. I'm dead beat."

"Alright," said the good-natured Rat. "You rest a while and get your strength back. I'll keep guard."

So the Mole laid down on the dry leaves and went to sleep. When he woke up, Ratty said, "I'll take a look outside and then we really must be off."

The Rat went to the entrance of their hollow tree and Mole heard him say, "Well I never!"

"What's up Ratty?" asked the Mole.

"Snow is up," replied the Rat briefly. "Or rather down! It's snowing hard.

"We must make a start," he said. "The worst of it is, I don't know exactly where we are."

The two friends set out bravely, but after just an hour they realised they were hopelessly lost. They pulled up, downhearted, weary and terribly cold.

They were aching and bruised with tumbles, they had fallen into several holes and got wet through. The snow was getting so deep that they could hardly drag their legs through it.

"We can't sit here very long," said the Rat. "We must try to find a cave or a hole with a dry floor, out of the wind and the snow!"

So once more they got to their feet and struggled on through the whirling snow, when suddenly, Mole tripped up and fell forward on his face with a groan. "Oh my leg," he cried. "Oh my poor shin!" He sat up on the snow and nursed his leg in both front paws. "I must have tripped over a hidden branch or a stump," went on the Mole miserably.

"That was never done by a branch or stump," said Ratty, examining Moley's leg. "Looks as if it was made of a sharp metal edge. Funny!"

"It hurts just the same, whatever did it!" cried Mole as the Rat tied up the leg with a handkerchief.

Then to Mole's surprise, the Rat began to scratch and shovel the snow. Suddenly, the Rat cried, "Hooray! Hooray! Come and see what I've found!"

The Mole hobbled up to the spot and had a good look...just peeping above the snow was a door scraper!

The Rat set to work once more, digging deep in the snow and he discovered...a doormat!

As quickly as he could, Ratty attacked the snow bank beside them with his stick.

After ten minutes, the point of Ratty's stick struck something that sounded hollow. Faster and harder they dug, until, in full view of the astonished Mole, a solid looking door appeared.

It was painted dark green. An iron bell hung by the side and below it on a small brass plate, neatly written, were the words, 'Mr Badger'.

Mole fell backwards on the snow from sheer surprise and delight. "Ratty! I can't believe it!" he cried.

"Get up at once and hang on to that bell pull," ordered Ratty. "Ring as hard as you can, while I hammer."

While the Rat attacked the door with his stick, the Mole sprang up at the bell pull and swung from there. From a long way off, they could faintly hear a deep toned bell and a while later, the sound of slow, shuffling footsteps.

There was the noise of a bolt shooting back and
the door opened a few inches. "Now, who is it
disturbing people on such a night?" said a gruff voice.

"Oh Badger," cried Ratty, "let us in please. It's
me, Ratty. Mole and I have lost our way in the snow."

"Why Ratty, my dear little man!" exclaimed the
Badger, in quite a different voice, "Come in, both of
you. You must be frozen through!"

The Badger looked down at them kindly and patted their heads. "This is not the sort of night for small animals to be out," he said. "Come into the kitchen, there's a first rate fire there, and supper and everything."

He shuffled on in front of them, carrying the light, and they followed him down a long gloomy passage, until they came to several stout doors. Badger flung open one of them and beckoned them through. At once, they found themselves in all the glow and warmth of a fire lit kitchen.

The floor was well-worn red brick, and on the wide hearth there was a blazing log fire with a couple of high backed seats on either side.

"Sit down and toast yourselves!" said Badger.

Then he made them take off their wet coats and boots and he fetched them dressing gowns and slippers.

Warm and dry at last, it seemed that the Wild Wood they had just left outside was miles and miles away.

When at last they were thoroughly warm, the Badger called them to the table where he had been busy laying a meal.

He sat in his armchair at the head of the table as they ate their supper. Then he listened as Ratty and Mole told of their adventures in the Wild Wood. Mole began to think the Badger was really very friendly.

After supper, they chatted some more by the fireside. Then Badger noticed how worn out Ratty was.

"It's time we were in bed," said Badger, getting up and fetching candlesticks. He led the animals to a long room where he kept all his winter stores. There were piles of apples, turnips, potatoes, nuts and jars of honey. But most appealing were the two small beds by the wall, which Ratty and Mole soon tumbled into.

When the Rat and Mole emerged the next morning, they found two young hedgehogs sitting at the table eating porridge.

"Did you youngsters lose your way in the snow as well?" the Rat chuckled.

"Yes sir," said the elder hedgehog. "The weather out there is terribly bad."

Suddenly, the front door bell rang loudly, and Ratty sent the smaller hedgehog to answer it.

There was the sound of stamping in the hall and soon the Otter appeared. He was delighted to see that Ratty and Mole were safe.

"Thought I'd find you here alright," said the Otter cheerfully. "Everyone on the river bank was very worried about you both," the Otter went on. "'Ratty never been home all night, nor Mole either, something dreadful must have happened,' they said, and the snow had covered up all your tracks.

"I was going through the snow when I met a rabbit sitting on a stump. He was such a silly fellow, I had to cuff him round the ears to get any sense out of him. He did say he'd seen Mole though, so I knew I was on the right track."

"Weren't you at all...er...nervous?" asked the Mole remembering yesterday's terror in the Wild Wood.

"Nervous?" the Otter said, showing a shiny set of white teeth as he laughed. "I'd give 'em nerves if they tried it on with me. Here, Mole, fry me some ham. I'm starving and I've got a lot to say to Ratty, haven't seen him for ages!"

Badger, who had been asleep in his study, was pleased to see the Otter and invited him to lunch.

"Here, you two youngsters, be off home to your mother!" said Badger to the two young hedgehogs, as he gave them sixpence each and sent them on their way.

All during that morning the four friends talked and talked. After lunch, Otter and Ratty settled down to chat about their beloved river bank while Badger lit a lantern and took Mole on a tour down the dim passages of his underground home.

Now Mole was an underground animal and Badger's house suited him exactly, but not Ratty!

When they got back to the kitchen, they found him walking up and down, very restless, longing to get back to his river bank.

"Stop fretting Ratty," said Badger. "My passages run further than you think. In fact some of them run beneath the wood, right to the very edge."

The Rat was eager to be off, so Badger took his lantern and led the way through a maze of tunnels, until, at last, they saw daylight at the end of the passage.